W9-BEN-462

Illustrations by Romain Simon
Text by Rosalind Sutton

BABOU the baby elephant

BRIMAX BOOKS CAMBRIDGE ENGLAND

Babou the baby elephant, was born in Africa in a forest bordering the savannah — the hot grasslands. He was grey, hairy and had very big ears. His grandmother, Simbala, led the herd, guarding it from danger.

The yellow baboons, who like to see everything, watched the herd. The elephants had been feeding nearly all night; eating grass, leaves, twigs and branches. They use their trunks to gather the food and put it into their mouths. These large animals need enormous meals; they strip an area of its vegetation and then move on to find more. Babou gripped his mother's tail with his trunk. They couldn't hold hands, could they? "Come," she said, "keep close! I don't want to lose you!" They started off. Elephants move silently. Babou knew how to walk as if on rubber pads!

Elephants have poor sight. If this big bird, the hornbill, kept still they wouldn't notice it. Their sense of smell, however, is excellent. They lift their trunks up into the wind and can tell exactly who is about. Their hearing is good too. Babou's big ears picked up the slightest sound. He flapped them, cooling himself, driving off the tormenting insects. On and on trooped the herd across the scorching plain.

HORNBILL

At last: there was the river. They bathed and wallowed in the mud. Babou rolled over and over. His insect bites felt better. It was wonderful! A fierce warthog was enjoying a drink. Long-legged birds waded; fishing and prodding. One caught a small snake. It was the secretary bird. That name was given because the head-feathers look like quill or feather pens. Long ago, secretaries used feather pens and poked them behind the ear. A stork flew over but Babou didn't notice. He only wanted rest — and the mud! Simbala looked round smelling for danger. A hungry lion might be hidden; waiting to attack a helpless baby elephant.

WARTHOG

SECRETARY BIRD

Babou showered and splashed! Bathing-time was the best part of the day. Not far off, Madam Hippopotamus pretended to be asleep; she didn't want to be disturbed. She spent her days lazing in the water and her nights grazing on land. The yellow-billed stork, or wood ibis waited for a fish. Babou; he just enjoyed himself.

PELICAN

The elephants had left the river; but Babou could not climb the slippery bank. The mud sucked him in as he tried to move. He was frightened. The little egrets with white lacy feathers, they were worried too. The pelican and crowned cranes watched his struggles. At last, his mother pushed him. "Up, Babou! Try again, up!" Her great strength saved him.

One afternoon, when Simbala and the herd were having a snooze under the cool mimosa trees, Babou took himself off. 'I'm not sleepy! I'll have an adventure!' he thought. Suddenly, there in front of him a stranger appeared with a sharp horn on his nose! He was terrible and so cross!

He was more than cross — he was furious! ‘Who was this stupid baby elephant, disturbing him? . . . How dare he!’ thought the rhinoceros. Babou didn’t know what to do. He had never seen such an animal; he had never been so alone.

The rhinoceros scraped the ground, making a cloud of dust; showing his anger. Then he charged! Babou took to his heels. He did not see the beautiful goliath beetle. He was away! Only speed could save him.

GOLIATH BEETLE

When they reached the herd Rhino made off. “Trust no one!” said Babou’s mother. “And never leave the herd. Your tusks must grow; then you may go alone.”

Babou was learning many things about life on the savannah. He saw Father Lion with his handsome mane and the lioness and her cub, all golden coloured like the dried grasses. Zebras made him chuckle with their dazzling stripes and small wagging tails. He watched the gazelles, so timid and so swift. They always disappeared before the flesh-eating animals, the lions, leopards and hyenas, started their evening hunt.

Simbala wasn't afraid of any hunters. When elephants and lions meet they take no notice of each other. It is only when a disobedient baby elephant strays or lags behind that a lion would be tempted to attack. Any animal trying to steal Babou from the herd would be trampled to death by the angry elephants.

Babou was excited. He'd found a mountain — a termite hill! Termites, or white ants aren't really like ants. They tunnel underground; then cement their runs with the waste from their bodies. Babou was 'King of the Castle' — he danced and trumpeted! It was fun! Termites dislike daylight so they didn't swarm over him. Babou's mother and aunt were watching. Sometimes elephants dig into termite hills to eat the cement, or clay, for its salt. They need salt to keep healthy.

One day, Babou was being very good and keeping out of mischief. Suddenly, he came across a young chimpanzee. It was quite alone and no mother in sight. Babou was delighted with his new friend. But Simbala was annoyed; she thought Babou might follow the ape and be in danger. Babou was enjoying the fun. He liked the faces Chimpy pulled and his clever antics. Simbala wasn't amused: she was angry!

She stretched out her big ears!
Yes, she was very angry.
"Come back!" she ordered.
Poor Babou, he hadn't been naughty! As for Chimpy, he was terrified and disappeared into the bushes.

Here is Babou when he tried to be as clever as his mother. He'd seen her up-root trees — easily. So, he could too! He chose one he liked, about the right size, rolled his trunk round and pulled. Next, he was sprawling; holding the broken piece!

While Babou had been busy, three buffaloes had come close behind him. Now wild African buffaloes are fierce and among the most dangerous animals on the savannah. But these just stood gazing! Why was that? They knew Simbala and her herd were near by: Babou was safe!

One evening, the elephants were lifting their trunks breathing in a delicious smell — bananas! "Hmmm!" said Simbala, "We'll go!" Later, in darkness and silence they found the plantation. What a feast!

Babou was having a wonderful time. Suddenly, Simbala signalled: "Out!" The cattle, a domesticated variety of zebu, had smelt them and were restless. The herd had to go, or there'd be trouble.

Too late! The villagers made their attack; shouting and shooting arrows. The elephants went mad at the torches and all the hullabaloo. They stampeded; trampling plants, fences and sheds. Simbala dug in her tusks ripping off the thatching. It was terrifying!

Poor Babou! He was so bewildered. Dazzled by the torches and scared out of his wits, he ran and ran: but in the wrong direction! He couldn't see his mother or any of the herd. Out there, in the dark savannah he was all alone.

Yes, Babou was lost. Exhausted and miserable he sat down close to a big tree. It made him feel safer. The moon rose and shadows moved across the grasses. He heard hyenas laughing in the distance and the yapping of jackals. These two scavengers eat animals which have died or been killed by others.

Even so, a hyena with its strong jaws, might attack a baby elephant. Babou couldn't run any more. But he had learned never to turn his back to an enemy. He pressed closer to the tree. It felt like his mother's body, strong and comforting.

Babou remembered everything he'd learned. He knew that the leader would never give up searching for one of the herd who was lost or hurt. Yes, Simbala would come. She had picked up Babou's trail but was delayed by another danger. She could smell smoke!

Fire! It roared over the plain like a monster! Birds filled the sky. Animals fled for their lives: giraffes, gazelles, zebras, hyenas, jackals, leopards and lions. They weren't hunting or being hunted; all were racing from their worst enemy. Flames leapt towards

them; dry grasses blazed at their heels. If only they could reach the river! If only the rain would pour down! Babou had found enough strength to join the rush for safety but where were the others? Had the whole herd died in the fire?

No, wise Simbala had taken the mountain route. All were safe, and Babou was found! Waving his trunk he ambled along close to his mother. They roamed the hills finding fresh green food. One day new grasses would grow on the burnt-out plain. The elephants would return and Babou would have many more adventures.

FOR THOSE
WHO WOULD LIKE TO
KNOW MORE

The elephant is the largest land animal living today. Two species exist: Asian and African. The African is bigger; longer tusks and larger ears; measuring 3-4m. (9-12ft.) high; weighing 5,000-6,000 kg. (5-6 tons). Entirely vegetarian it eats grass, leaves, bark, branches, fruit and roots; 300 kg. (666lbs.) a day. It drinks morning and evening up to 180 litres (40 gals.) at one time, and feeds nearly all night. Its life span could reach 100 years — but seldom does.

Asian elephant

African elephant

Rudyard Kipling, who wrote the "Just-So Stories", told how the elephant got his trunk. But the first author to write of the animal was Herodotus, the Greek historian, 425 BC. Darius, King of Persia, used elephants to transport troops 500 BC. The elephant was first seen in Europe 280 BC. in wars against Romans. Hannibal of Carthage crossed the Alps into Italy 218 BC. in winter with his famous herd of elephants. He defeated the Romans. Asian elephants have worked for man for centuries. They are placid and can be trained. African elephants are difficult; wild and unpredictable.

Prehistoric man drew cave pictures of the elephant's ancestor: the mammoth. Fossils of this enormous animal have been found and in Siberia 1799, a whole mammoth, completely preserved in ice. Elephants have strong family feelings. The mother protects her baby (she has one at a time) keeping close, touching with her trunk, showing affection. It is 22 months after the mating before the baby is born. It weighs about 100kg. (222 lbs.) at birth. When a mother is going to have her baby the herd circles round to protect her. An aunt helps; then she, the mother and a young bull calf work for two hours getting the baby onto its feet. The baby takes milk from its mother (by mouth, not trunk) for three years; sometimes even longer. If a baby becomes an orphan, another mother in the herd adopts it. The elephant is adult at the age of fifteen.

The mammoth,
the elephant's ancestor
in prehistoric times.

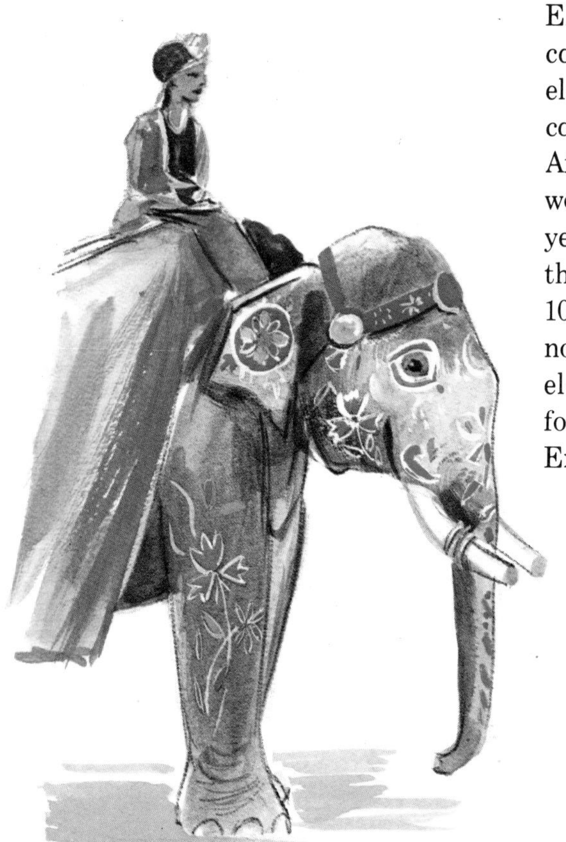

Elephants, richly robed and decorated, carried the Rajahs of India. Now, elephants work in the forests; each can carry a tree of 600kg. (over $\frac{1}{2}$ ton). In Africa, the only elephants trained to work are at Gangolana-Bodio. For years elephants have been hunted for their ivory tusks; one could weigh 100kg. (223lbs.). Law protects them now. The tusk is really a tooth. One elephant, 'the King' of Ituri Forest had four tusks. These can be seen in the Explorers' Club Museum, New York.

Here is a young Asian elephant trained for the circus. If he likes his trainer he is always gentle. Of all the animals, the elephant is the most difficult to train; taking a long time. Once he has learned, he remembers.

Elephants have short legs from knee to foot. They amble along; moving both legs on one side together; then both on the other side together. Camels, bears and giraffes walk in this way. An elephant needs gallons of water every day. He will walk great distances to find it. In a drought he'll dig in the dried river-bed and wait for water to seep into his hole. Bathing is important to the elephant. He is a good swimmer and loves a shower from his trunk. He enjoys a dust bath too. He has excellent hearing and sense of smell: his sight is weak. A young elephant has four teeth; one each side of top and bottom jaws. As these wear down others grow to replace them; this can happen six times. When the last set has worn away he can no longer chew: he starves to death.

An angry elephant can charge at more than 40km. (over 25 miles) an hour. The ears are spread wide and the tusks held out straight for the attack. When an elephant is wounded, others of the herd stand by to help: or wait for it to die. When young bull elephants grow up the cow elephants turn them out of the family group. They may stay just outside or wander off to join other bulls. The bulls like to be near other elephants so they move around the family groups, visiting them at breeding times. They do not help to bring up the calves.

Elephants show affection to one another with their trunks. On meeting other groups they touch and wave their trunks—quite a ceremony of greeting.